VOLCANOES

SALLY COWAN

Australia • Brazil • Japan • Korea • Mexico • Singapore • Spain • United Kingdom • United States

Volcanoes

Text: Sally Cowan
Editor: Rochelle Ransom
Design: Jess Kelly
Series design: James Lowe
Photo researcher: Lisa Piemonte
Production controllers: Renee Cusmano and Lisa Porter
Reprint: Jennifer Foo

Acknowledgements
The author and publisher would like to acknowledge permission to reproduce material from the following sources:
Andrew Young: p. 16; Getty Images: 9, 15, back cover;
Guy Holt © Cengage Learning Australia: pp. 5, 22–23;
Ingo Arndt/Naturepl.com: pp. 1, 12, cover;
iStockphoto/Craig Hansen: p. 13; iStockphoto/Graeme Knox: p. 17;
NASA: p. 19; Phil Kelly: p. 18 (top); Photolibrary: pp. 3–4, 6 (bottom), 7–8, 10–11, 20–21; Photolibrary/The Bridgeman Art Library: p. 23 (inset); Steven David Miller/Naturepl.com: p. 14; USGS/Cascades Volcano Observatory: p. 5; Victoria Kelly: p. 18 (bottom).

Every effort has been made to trace and acknowledge copyright. However, if any infringement has occurred, the publishers tender their apologies and invite the copyright holders to contact them.

Fast Forward Independent Texts
Level 19

For product information and technology assistance,
in Australia call 1300 790 853;
in New Zealand call 0508 635 766

For permission to use material from this text or product,
please email **aust.permissions@cengage.com**

ISBN 978 0 17 018100 6
ISBN 978 0 17 017898 3 (set)

Cengage Learning Australia
Level 7, 80 Dorcas Street
South Melbourne, Victoria Australia 3205

Cengage Learning New Zealand
Unit 4B Rosedale Office Park
331 Rosedale Road, Albany, North Shore NZ 0632

For learning solutions, visit **cengage.com.au**

Printed in Australia by Ligare Pty Ltd
3 4 5 6 7 8 9 21 20 19 18 17

VOLCANOES

SALLY COWAN

Contents

CHAPTER 1

How Volcanoes Work

Volcanoes are found at places in Earth's **crust** where **lava**, rock, ash and gases escape to the surface.

A layer of hot liquid rock is found deep inside Earth.
Sometimes the liquid rock melts the layer of hot rock under Earth's crust.

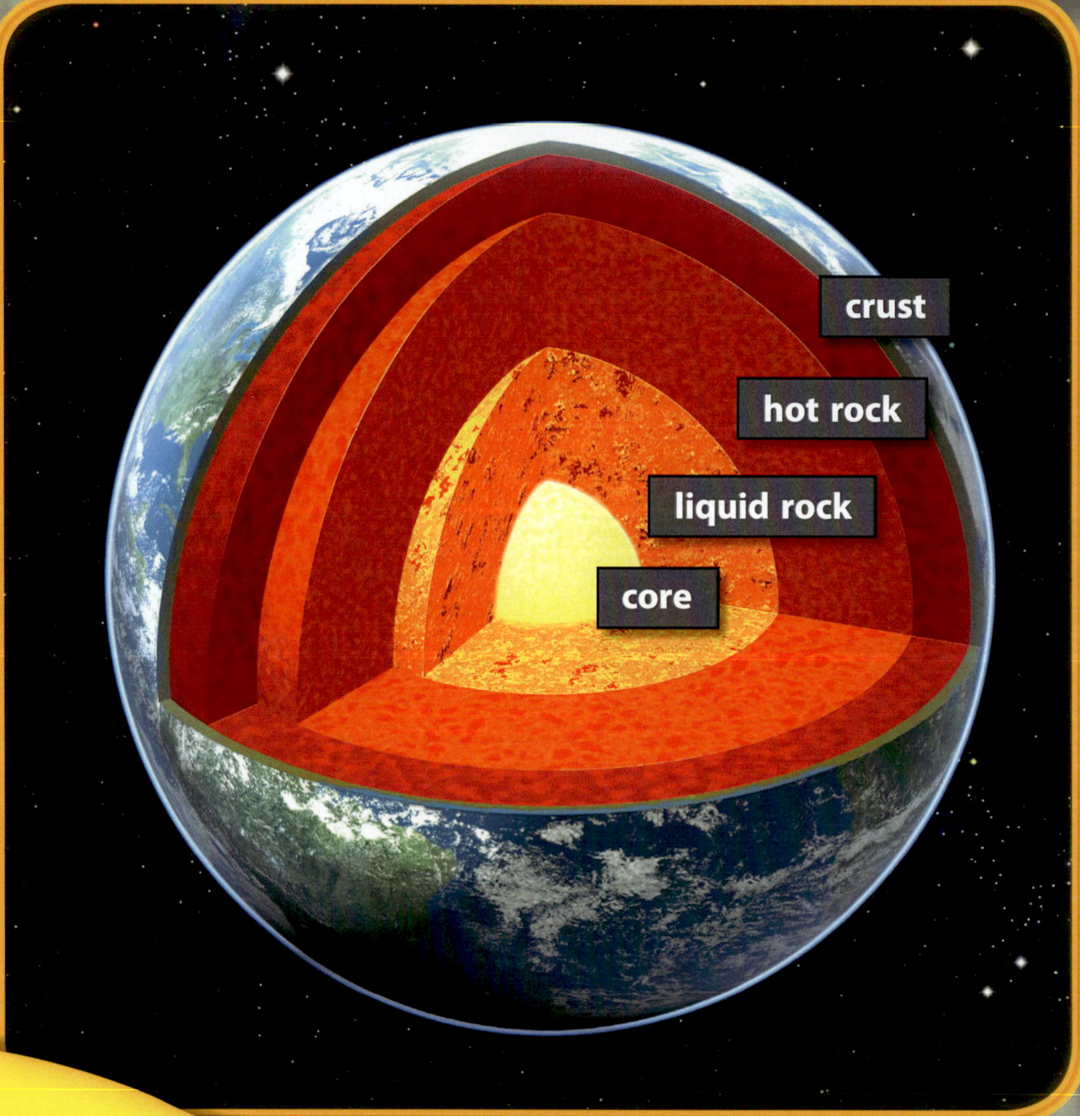

When there is a crack in the crust,
the lava moves up and out onto the surface,
making a volcano.
This is called an eruption.

Mount St Helens, USA, 1980

Kinds of Eruptions

Mild eruptions,
where lava flows out slowly,
form low, wide volcanoes.

Mount Edziza, Canada

Strong eruptions,
where rocks, lava and ash are thrown into the air
then land on the sides of the volcano,
build cone-shaped volcanoes.

Mount Mayon, the Philippines

Some large volcanoes erupt with so much force that the land around the edge of the volcano collapses and sinks into the hole left behind by the eruption.

Caldera Blanca, Lanzarote, Canary Islands

Finding Volcanoes

Earth's crust is made up of huge pieces called plates. Most volcanoes are found in the cracks between the plates, because it is easy for the liquid rock to find its way to the surface.

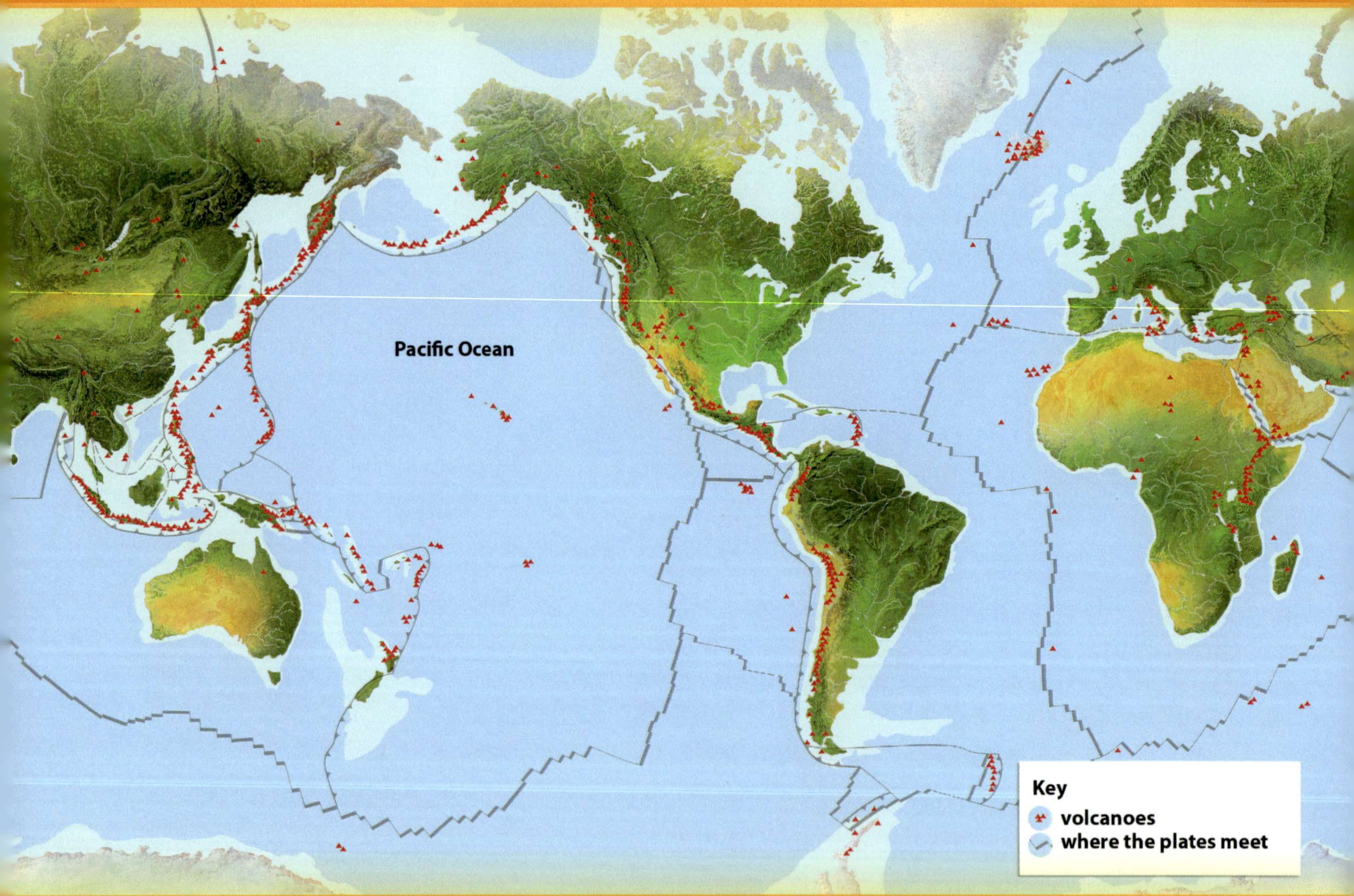

Pacific Ocean

Key
volcanoes
where the plates meet

Volcano Fact

There are so many volcanoes around the edges of the Pacific Ocean that it is called the Ring of Fire.

Sometimes, volcanoes form in the middle of plates, over hot spots. Hot spots are formed when heat wells up from deep inside Earth and makes an area of liquid rock so hot that it melts a hole in the crust and forms a volcano.

The volcanoes of Hawaii were formed over a hot spot.

Underwater Volcanoes

Many volcanoes are under the sea. Not long ago, scientists discovered some huge active volcanoes about a kilometre under the sea, near Fiji. Two of the volcanoes are around 4000 metres tall.

Sometimes, underwater volcanoes form islands.
In 1963, an island suddenly appeared
off the coast of Iceland.
It had formed from a volcanic eruption
that piled lava, ash and rocks up above sea level.

Surtsey Island, Iceland

Active, Dormant or Extinct

Volcanoes can be active, dormant or extinct. Active volcanoes erupt or show signs that they could erupt.

Stromboli in Italy is one of the most active volcanoes on Earth.

Dormant volcanoes have not erupted for hundreds or even thousands of years, but scientists believe that they could erupt in the future.

Mount Fuji in Japan is a dormant volcano.

Extinct volcanoes have not erupted for thousands of years and show no signs of ever erupting again.

The Blue Lake in South Australia has formed in the crater of an extinct volcano.

Sometimes, it is hard to know whether a volcano is extinct or just dormant.

The Chaiten volcano in Chile was believed to be extinct, until it erupted in May 2008.

CHAPTER 4

Mount Ruapehu: Living Near a Volcano

Jess grew up in New Zealand.
Here, she talks about living near Mount Ruapehu, one of the world's most active volcanoes.

Jess, November 2008

The first thing I remember about Mount Ruapehu was my dad telling me about a terrible train accident that happened there in 1953. A ***mudslide*** *came down the volcano and washed away part of a train bridge. The train then fell into the mud.*

Mount Ruapehu has ski fields.
One winter, I was looking forward to going skiing there with friends in the school holidays.
But we couldn't go because the volcano was active and the ski field was closed.

My dad drives a truck along the Desert Road,
which passes by Mount Ruapehu.
The road was closed twice last year,
so he had to turn back both times.
In March, a mudslide came down the volcano.
Then in September, a small eruption caused a thick fog of ash,
which made driving dangerous.

Jess's dad, Phil, and his truck near Mount Ruapehu

a satellite photograph of Mount Ruapehu

Volcano Fact

Mudslides from volcanoes are called lahars. Ash and rock from the volcano mix with water to make a thick mud, like concrete. Lahars can be dangerously fast and powerful.

The New Zealand Government has just put out a warning that Mount Ruapehu is active again.

Studying Volcanoes

Scientists learn a lot from past eruptions. They have studied the eruption of Mount Vesuvius in Italy in 79 AD, which buried the city of Pompeii in ash. Thousands of people died.

plaster cast models of the victims of the Mount Vesuvius eruption in Pompeii

Scientists who **monitor** Mount Vesuvius today believe that another strong eruption could happen in the future. But this time, because of the shape of the volcano, an eruption could send clouds of ash and poisonous gases over the city of Naples.

Unlike in 79 AD, there would be time to give people warning to **evacuate**.

Scientists also study changes to the climate caused by past eruptions.

In 1815, the biggest eruption in modern times happened at Mount Tambora in Indonesia. Dust, ash, carbon dioxide and other gases were thrown high into the atmosphere and blocked the Sun for days.

Volcano Fact

Some scientists are studying the colours of sunsets in nineteenth century paintings to work out how much dust was thrown into the air by volcanic eruptions.

By 1816, the effects were felt as far away as Europe, China and North America. People called it "the year without a summer".

This kind of study helps scientists to understand more about climate change, global warming and volcanoes.

Glossary

crust the thin outer layer of Earth

evacuate leave a dangerous place to find safety

lava hot liquid rock that comes out of volcanoes

monitor keep track of

mudslide a large amount of mud that moves down a slope

Index